About the Author

My passion and expertise has always been through my career working with children and also by being a very proud mum myself. I have been able to combine my knowledge of children with my love of writing to create stories that young children will find thoroughly enjoyable and very relatable. My *Cheeky Chappie* stories have been developed through the inspiration created by my experiences with children as well as the daily adventures and memorable moments that I am privileged to share with my beloved animal friends, which are of course very much part of my family and hold a special place in my heart.

Cheeky Chappie the Superhero

Louise Jesson

Cheeky Chappie the Superhero

Nightingale Books

A CIP catalogue record for this title is
available from the British Library.
ISBN 9781838751302

Nightingale Books is an imprint of
Pegasus Elliot MacKenzie Publishers Ltd.
www.pegasuspublishers.com

First Published in 2021

Nightingale Books
Sheraton House Castle Park
Cambridge England

Printed & Bound in Great Britain

Dedication

For my husband, Tony, and my two daughters, Erin and Anna. With all my love and appreciation for your continued support and encouragement. And of course thank you to Chappie for always being my little superhero.

I hope that you enjoy my book and please remember that as amazing as us chameleons are we are exotic creatures and take a lot of specialist care and know how, as we can be very tricky and extremely cheeky!

Cheeky Chappie had woken up this morning full of energy, in fact he was a... *radiant orange* colour. This was all because he had been given the most spectacular of superhero costumes and today was the day to transform into CHAPPIE THE COURAGEOUS!

As soon as Chappie put on the costume he felt like he had turned into the most strongest, fastest, and courageous of chameleons. "**Chappie the Courageous to the rescue!**" shouted Chappie, in his loudest of superhero voices.

Cheeky Chappie zoomed from out of his bedroom and **straight** into Mummy Chameleon, who was coming up the stairs carrying an enormous pile of freshly ironed clothes.

Oh dear, there were clothes everywhere! Chappie could see Mummy's favourite dress dangling down from the chandelier, Daddy's smart shirt was hanging from the picture frame, Chappie's best T-shirt was sliding down the banister and just when Chappie thought that it couldn't get any worse, Granny Chameleon then walked out of her bedroom with a pair of Chappie's pants on top of her head!

"**Chappieeeee**, I have just spent the past hour ironing and folding all that clean washing and now look, they're scattered everywhere and even on poor Granny's head. Chappie, you should know not to go running about in the house, you could hurt yourself or someone else," Mummy said in her very cross voice.

Chappie felt a little silly and shocked at the sight of all the washing, which had exploded everywhere, so much so that he quickly turned the colour... *pink*.

But then Chappie remembered that today he wasn't just ordinary Cheeky Chappie he was, Chappie the Courageous, and so it was time to act like a superhero. "You don't have to worry, Mum, you go and make yourself and Granny a nice cup of tea and I will pick up all these clothes," Chappie said in his big superhero voice.

Mummy Chameleon sighed and with Granny following, they went downstairs to leave Chappie to it. **"Chappie the Courageous to the rescue,"** he boomed and at superhero speed Chappie began to pick up all the clothes, flinging each item in turn as far and as high as possible towards each matching bedroom.

"That was easy," Chappie said using his deep superhero voice and then continued to zoom down the stairs and straight into the living room to find Granny Chameleon trying to untangle her knitting.

"Would you like me to help with that, Granny?"

Granny looked up from her knitting and said, "Well, only if you can be really careful, Chappie, you will need a steady hand and lots of patients."

"No problem, Granny, Chappie the Courageous can fix anything."

Granny looked a little unsure but left the living room to have her cup of tea. Cheeky Chappie began by carefully twisting and turning the lengths of wool in all directions but no matter what he did the tangle just seemed to get worse. "This is going to takes ages," groaned Chappie. "What I need is SUPER SPEED."

"Chappie the Courageous to the rescue!" At lightning speed Chappie began to pull, shake, fling and toss the knitting around the room, so much so that the knitting needles fell out and all Granny's knitting slowly started to unravel itself. What was the start of a beautiful knitted cardigan was now just a pile of wool.

Chappie looked at the wool and said, "That's it, I've fixed the tangle, Granny will be pleased." He then zoomed straight out the back door and into the garden to find Daddy Chameleon painting the summer house.

"Hi, Daddy, it's me, Chappie the Courageous, here to be of service, so why don't you let me finish the painting and you can take a nice break."

"Are you sure, Chappie? Painting can be hard work," questioned Daddy Chameleon.

"Not for Chappie the Courageous, now off you go."

Daddy Chameleon sighed but decided to take Chappie up on his offer and walked towards the house to have a break. Chappie began to paint, but as he started splashing the *brown* paint onto the summer house, he suddenly thought to himself, "How very boring, what this summer house needs is some colour!"

Chappie put the paint brush down and ran back into house to then return just a few minutes later, carrying a selection of his own brightly coloured paints. Chappie began to eagerly paint the summer house, while calling out, **"Chappie the Courageous to the rescue."**

Once Daddy Chameleon returned to check on Chappie he could not believe what he was seeing. The summer house was now a multi colour mix of spots, stripes, zig zags, splats and drips, there was every colour you could imagine running down each side of the summer house, creating *rainbow* puddles all over the lawn.

"**Chappieeeee,**" yelled Daddy. Chappie slowly appeared from around the back of the summer house, he took one look at Daddy's face then turned the colour... *grey*, with worry, now he was in big trouble!

"But I only wanted to help," pleaded Chappie in his not so brave voice.

Daddy Chameleon sat Chappie down and said, "Let me give you some good advice son, the best way to help someone is to really listen to what that person is wanting, and to help by doing the right thing."

"I'm sorry, Daddy, next time I really will listen and do what is right," he then gave his dad a great big chameleon cuddle, chameleons give the best cuddles.

"That's OK, Chappie, because even superhero's have to learn from their mistakes and you can start right now, by washing off all that runny paint and then finishing the painting using this lovely shade of brown and once you've done that, Granny will be waiting for you inside as you've got a cardigan to knit!"

Cheeky Chappie and Daddy Chameleon looked at each other and then burst into laughter. Chappie said, "OK, Daddy, I'm going to make things right." Chappie felt happy as this time he really did want to help and he was now all the... *colours of the rainbow*.